We've Got a Mission!

Designed by Carol Leslie & Nadeem Zaidi

Photo credits: Grand Roue ferris wheel © Owen Franken/Corbis; Meadow of daisies and wildflowers © Walter Geiersperger/Corbis; Clown fish between sea anemones © Tobias Bernhard/zefa/Corbis; School of orange fish following leader © Warren Morgan/Corbis; Red kangaroo with joey in pouch © Charles Philip Cangialosi/Corbis; Sea turtle swimming © Sunny S. Unal/Corbis; Ayers Rock and kangaroos, Australia © Otto Rogge/Corbis; Animal warning signs by the Eyre highway © Howard Davies/Corbis; Vegetation in front of Ayers Rock © Royalty-Free/Corbis; Tiger lying on ground © Royalty-Free/Corbis; Bengal tiger cubs perched on rock © Renee Lynn/Corbis; Siberian tiger running on snow © Royalty-Free/Corbis; Taj Mahal © Royalty-Free/Corbis; Robin redbreast flying (1) © H. Heintges/zefa/Corbis; Robin redbreast flying (2) © H. Heintges/zefa/Corbis; Fall color surrounding small town © Bob Krist/Corbis; Waits River, Vermont © Owaki-Kulla/Corbis; Home in affluent suburb © Ralph A. Clevenger/Corbis; Oak tree among lupines © Craig Aurness/Corbis; Watering can in low maintenance courtyard garden © Mark Bolton/Corbis; Purple corn cockle plants © Clay Perry/Corbis; Kremlin and Kremlin wall in Moscow, Russia © H. Spichtinger/zefa/Corbis; Hermitage Museum and Alexander Column © Jose Fuste Raga/Corbis; Gondolas in Venice © Myopia/Corbis; Metro sign on a streetlight © Nik Wheeler/Corbis; Emperor penguins © Tim Davis/Corbis; Wildlife grazing in the Serengeti National Park, Tanzania © Brian A. Vikander/Corbis; Elephants walking single file © Tim Davis/Corbis; Golden hills in Val d'Orcia—Tuscany, Italy © Bob Krist/Corbis; Roots and trunk of sloanea tree © Gary Braasch/Corbis; Mist rising in rain forest © Paul A. Souders/Corbis; Paradise Bay © Bob Krist/Corbis; St. Basil's Cathedral, Moscow, Russia © Janicek/Taxi; Costa Rica, Rara Avis Preserve, waterfall and rain forest © Stuart Westmorland/Stone; Keel-billed toucan (Ramphastos sulfuratus), Costa Rica © Schafer & Hill/Stone; Emperor penguins (Aptenodytes forsteri) standing in snow with chick © Pete Oxford/Taxi; Emperor penguin (Aptenodytes forsteri) with chick (digital composite) © Tim Davis/Photographer's Choice; Wildebeest herd approaching water hole, Chobe NP, Botswana © Daryl Balfour/Stone; USA, California, Joshua Tree National Park, desert scene © Arthur S. Aubry/Stone; Africa, Tanzania, Serengeti Plain, yellow barked acacia tree © Nicholas Parfitt/Stone; Capuchin monkey, Costa Rica © Philip Coblentz/Brand X Pictures; Thomson's gazelle (gazella thomsoni) running across plain © Photodisc Collection; Acacia Alveda © Jeremy Woodhouse/Photodisc Blue; African elephants reflected in water at Chobe National Park © Beverly Joubert/National Geographic; Kenya, Africa, zebra © Panoramic Images; Tree, Tsavo National Park, Kenya © Neil Emmerson/Robert Harding World Imagery; A scenic view of the Eiffel Tower on a sunny day © Todd Gipstein/National Geographic

ISBN 0-7868-5539-8
For more Disney Press fun, visit www.disneybooks.com

Mission:
Where's June?

by Susan Ring
Illustrated by Barrett Benica & Aram Song

France

Australia

Costa Rica

India

Russia

Antarctica

Africa